This book belongs to

....

The Mystery Glove

Nick and Claire Page

Illustrations by Cathy Shimmen

make
believe
ideas

Once upon a time, a young prince lived in a palace of snow and ice. The king and queen were not his real parents. All he had from his real mother was a single woolen glove she had made.

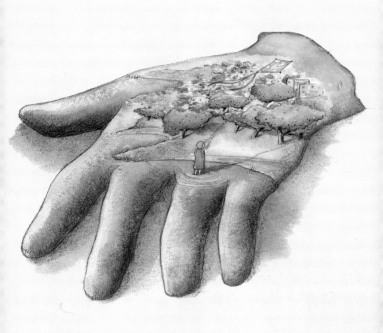

The glove showed a sandy beach, a
blue sea, and a golden girl flying a
kite. The prince kept the glove in his
pocket. When he touched it, he heard
music. It made him want to dance.
But he didn't.

The prince watched other children
laughing as they skated on the lake.
They laughed when they fell down.
There was always someone to help
them up again. It made him want
to skate. But he didn't.

Some days the prince went into the
forest and made tiny animals from
moss and twigs. He wanted to climb
the trees. But he didn't.

One day, he spotted a tent.
Inside sat an old man and his wife.
"Come in!" said the old woman.
"Sit here, close to the fire!"

The old woman was knitting a
coat the color of ice and fire.
"I have this glove," said the
prince. "Could you make
another?"

The woman shook her head.
"I can knit magic in fingers and
thumb, but I cannot repeat the work
that's been done. This can be made
only once."

The prince felt sad.

"Cheer up," said the old man.
He brought out a blue-and-white kite.
"Let's have a go!" he said. "Flying this
kite will make you warm."

14

The prince was nervous. But he held
the string tight, shut his eyes, and
threw the kite into the air.

The wind caught the kite. When the
prince opened his eyes, he was flying!

The kite took him up-up-up, over forest and mountains, and then down-down-down to a beautiful beach. Splash! He fell into the sea!

"Help! I can't swim!" he yelled.
Then someone reached down and
lifted him onto a rock. It was a
golden girl, and she was laughing.

On her right hand, the girl wore a glove. It showed a palace, children skating, and a boy wrapped in furs.

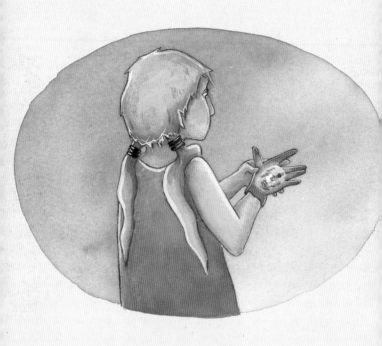

"You know me," said the girl.
The prince looked at his glove
and then at the girl.
"I'm your sister!" she said, smiling.

They talked about their lives.

"If I had your sunshine," the prince said,
"I would always be happy and brave."

"And if I had your snow," the golden girl
said, "I'd be thoughtful and wise."

They pressed their hands together. They looked the same, but his was cold and hers was warm. Together, they threw the blue kite into the air, and flew back to the tent in the woods.

But the old couple were nowhere to be seen.

20

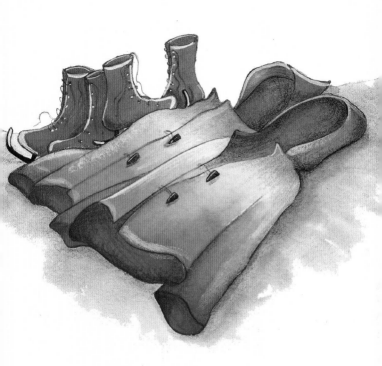

Two coats, the color of ice and
fire, lay by the door of the tent,
with two pairs of skates.
"Teach me to skate!" said the
golden girl.

So they put their coats on and
rushed onto the lake. A chain of
children became a circle of friends.

The prince heard music. It made him
feel happy and brave. When it stopped,
everyone fell down and laughed. The
prince looked up but the girl was gone.

She was high up, waving
good-bye from the kite.
"Next time we meet, you must
teach me to swim!" he shouted.
He turned to his friends, with
the glove on his hand.

And as he skated towards them,
the prince heard the music of summer.

Ready to tell

Oh no! Some of the pictures from this story have been mixed up! Can you retell the story and point to each picture in the correct order?

27

Picture dictionary

Encourage your child to read these words
from the story and gradually develop his
or her basic vocabulary.

coat

forest

friends

glove

kite

knitting

skate

snow

tent

Key words

Here are some key words used in context.
Help your child to use other words from the
border in simple sentences.

The prince watched the children.

He made tiny animals.

She was his sister.

They pressed their
hands together.

They put their coats **on**.

Create a cool kite

It is hard to make a kite that can really fly. But why not make one to hang on the wall of your room?

You will need

strong paper, 40 in (101 cm) x 40 in (101 cm) • two thin sticks or canes, 24 in (50 cm) long and 36 in (70 cm) long • ruler • pencil • scissors • strong sticky tape • paints, pens, or crayons • colored ribbons or tinsel • string

What to do

1 Lay the sticks on a flat surface in the shape of a cross. Use sticky tape to join them in the middle. (Ask a grown-up to help.)
2 Lay the stick frame on the paper. Make a pencil mark 1 in (2.5 cm) out from the end of each stick. Remove frame.
3 Draw lines to join the pencil marks to make a diamond shape. Cut along these lines.
4 Decorate one side of the paper with crayons or paint (let it dry).
5 Turn the paper over and tape the stick frame in place.
6 Add a long tail on the kite using string, ribbon, or tinsel. Then tie more ribbons or tinsel to the tail. Now your kite is ready to hang on the wall!